WHAT WOULD Y★U WISH FOR?

DAVID SABLE & EMMA YARLETT

Z|**ZONDERkidz**

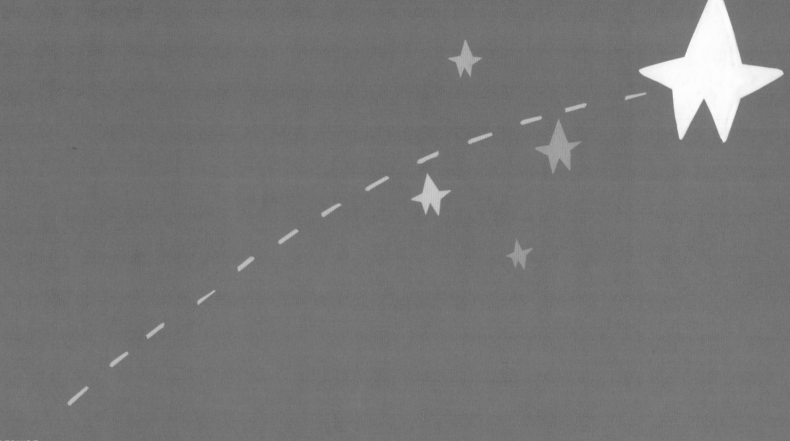

ZONDERKIDZ

What Would You Wish For?
Copyright © 2020 by David Sable
Illustrations © 2020 by Emma Yarlett

Requests for information should be addressed to:
Zonderkidz, 3900 *Sparks Drive SE, Grand Rapids, Michigan 49546*

Hardcover ISBN 978-0-310-76885-2
Ebook ISBN 978-0-310-76887-6

Art direction and design: Ron Huizinga

Printed in China

20 21 22 23 /DSC/ 22 21 20 19 18 17 16 15 14 13 12 11 10 9 8 7 6 5 4 3 2 1

When God told King Solomon that he could ask for anything and his wish would
be granted, King Solomon said, "I want a 'Lev Shomea'"—a Listening Heart.
To my grandchildren: Henry, Teddy, Gemma, Goldy, and Sadie.
May you all be granted listening hearts to help change the world.
—D. S.

For the Randall Family (and your Rainbows!)
With all my love,
—E

If you had some wishes
that were just for you,
What would you wish for?

What would you do . . .
if all of your wishes could
really come true?

You could wish for a ship,

a bike,

or a car.

Or wait! You might wish to become . . .

a movie star!

Would you like
a big monster under your bed?

Or maybe a fiery dragon instead?

You could wish for your very own ice cream maker!

AND (while you're at it)

how about a personal cookie baker?

You could wish it were your birthday,

not just today,

But next week and tomorrow

and every day!

You could wish for some snow to slide in and play
And ride on your favorite one-horse sleigh.

And instead of having to clean
your own room,
You could wish for . . .

an elf

or a robot

or bear
with a duster and broom!

Would you wish for some
dress-up clothes like these?

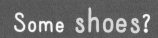

Some **shoes?**

Or a hat?

No need to say "Please!"

You could wish for puppies, a personal clown . . .

and the

BIGGEST,

MEANEST

fort in town.

Or maybe

you'd want

something else

instead.

You might wish that nobody
went to bed feeling hungry or thirsty . . .

or lonely and sad . . .

or feeling incredibly, awfully bad.

Maybe you'd wish for peace, love, and joy
for every single girl and boy.

If you had some wishes just for you,
What would you wish for?